▲ TIME TO LOVE

STORIES FROM THE

OLD TESTAMENT

BY WALTER DEAN MYERS

WITH ARTWORK BY

CHRISTOPHER MYERS

A TIME TO LOVE

SCHOLASTIC PRESS   NEW YORK

Text copyright © 2003 by Walter Dean Myers

Illustrations copyright © 2003 by Christopher Myers

Preface copyright © 2003 by Michael Dean Myers

Library of Congress Cataloging-in-Publication Data

Myers, Walter Dean, 1937–

A time to love: stories from the Old Testament / written by Walter Dean Myers;

illustrated by Christopher Myers. — 1st ed.

p. cm.

Summary: A retelling of six stories from the Old Testament, which explore the complexities of love from the perspectives of Delilah, Ruth, Reuben, Isaac, Zillah, and Aser.

ISBN 0-439-22000-9

1. Bible. O.T. — History of Biblical events — Juvenile fiction. [1. Bible. O.T. — History of Biblical events — Fiction. 2. Short stories.] I. Myers, Christopher A., ill. II. Title.

PZ7.M992 Ti 2002

[Fic] — dc21

2001043466

10 9 8 7 6 5 4 3 2 1   03 04 05 06 07

Printed in Singapore 46

First edition, April 2003

The display type was set in Constructivist Solid.

The text type was set in 14-point Monotype Pastonchi.

Book design by David Saylor

For Ethel, Imogene, and Viola,
my sisters, my friends — W. D. M.

ACKNOWLEDGMENTS

With special thanks to Dr. Charles E. Carter of Seton Hall University,
Associate Professor and Chair of the Department of Religious Studies, for
his careful reading of the manuscript. — W. D. M.

This book took a lot of work, work that I was thrilled, excited, and daunted
by. It never would have been completed were it not for several people who
deserve more thanks than I can give them. Thank you so much to: Kerry-
Anne Ryce-Paul, Aysha Somasundaram, Roxanne Ryce-Paul, Abeni
Crooms, Sumitra Rajkumar, Kambui Olujimi, John Whitlow, Micheline
Brown, Begay Downes-Thomas, Miriam Neptune, Linda Mboya, Althea
Wasow, Nnenna Lynch, Walter Myers, and especially Constance Myers,
my mother, who took me with her to holy places like church and museums,
who taught me about God and art, who taught me how to love. (She's also a
really good hand model.) — C. M.

CONTENTS

PREFACE

by Chaplain, Captain, Michael Dean Myers

GROWING UP in a religious community, as well as a religious family, I was exposed to the Bible at an early age. I was also exposed to the various interpretations of the stories in the Bible. When my feelings toward Christianity intensified in my early teens, I sensed a need to learn for myself exactly what the Bible taught, so I began my journey through the Scriptures.

The Authorized King James Version of the Bible proved to be a formidable task. I found myself using three books: the family Bible, a dictionary, and a children's picture Bible, to get a better feel for the times and atmosphere. I eventually grew to love reading the stories and imagining myself back in those fabled times. It was that love for reading and understanding the Scriptures that eventually led to my call to the ministry. To this day, people tell me that I have an interesting and insightful view of the Scriptures. This helps them understand God better, as well as His direction for their lives. I frequently recall those early days of exploring the Bible, allowing my imagination to run wild — putting myself into the stories and making the experiences of God's people relevant to myself.

When I first read my father's book, *A Time to Love*, I discovered that he, as a writer, was doing the same thing that I had done, absorbing these stories into his imagination and making them his own. As a pastor, I'm constantly trying to find fresh and exciting ways to present the Scriptures to people. *A Time to Love* does just that — telling classic Biblical stories in an accurate way, but with a different twist, from a unique perspective. For instance, normally we'd hear the story of Abraham from a narrator's perspective, or from Abraham's — what must have been going through his mind, the internal struggle he must have gone through as he prepared to sacrifice Isaac. But my father tells the story through the eyes of an anxious son, going up the mountain wondering where the sacrifice was. He tells the story of Joseph, who was sold into slavery, through the eyes of a frustrated, guilt-ridden, yet loving older brother, Reuben. The distant, mythical stories become immediate, the characters become wonderfully human.

Staying true to the spirit of the text is important to me. *A Time to Love* does this, yet adds much more by emphasizing the human element and correlating the spiritual element of faith with life's circumstances. We all have vari-

ous challenges presented to us throughout our lives. My

father reminds us that God *is* love, and the way to face life's

challenges, and the best expression of our faith, regardless

of the denomination on the house of worship, is through

love.

X

INTRODUCTION

by Walter Dean Myers

STORIES FROM THE BIBLE have always been a part of my life. As a four-year-old in Harlem, I loved hearing the stories in Sunday school at Abyssinian Baptist. A few years later my older sister, Geraldine, gave me a book of Bible stories that she had been given as a child. The stories were, as I remember them, all from the Old Testament and illustrated with heavy woodcuts. I loved the drama of the stories and the absolute sense of good and evil. I was also convinced that I was good.

At eight years of age I was attending The Church of the Master. The church played a central role in my life, encompassing many different activities. I learned to play basketball in the church gym, made wallets and plastic lanyards in summer Bible school, and took Monday night Bible Study classes. When the youth division sponsored a dance recital, I found myself in the role of Adam in a dance created around James Weldon Johnson's "The Creation." I loved dancing, and I loved bringing this story from the book of Genesis to life.

But my most influential encounter with Bible stories came in my early teen years, when my grandfather came to live with us. Pap was a tall, rather stern-looking man, whose voice would lift and swell with emotion as he told stories of a vengeful and unforgiving God. The basic theme of my grandfather's stories seemed clear enough: If you messed up, God was going to get you. My grandfather had a story ready for each and every occasion. I quickly became his favorite audience.

If I came home with a complaint about my school day, he would remind me of how Job had suffered without complaining. If I bragged about a good grade, he would remind me of the false pride of those who had built the tower of Babel. In my grandfather's way of telling the stories, God became pretty scary.

I became interested in reading the Bible in my mid-teens, and my impressions were different from those of my grandfather. Where he saw a constantly angry God dealing with faceless mortals known only for their good or bad deeds, I saw men and women struggling to understand their relationships with one another and with a Higher Being. Where my grandfather could look at the destruction of Sodom and Gomorrah with a kind of self-righteous satisfaction, I worried about the people being destroyed and was more than a bit put out with what seemed to be a very minor transgression by Lot's wife. I wondered why she had looked back. What was she thinking? Could I have made that mistake?

When I began to write, the stories I put down on paper were often stories that had captured my imagination as a child, including the Old Testament stories. I saw the stories as vastly more complex than the way Pap had told them. Much later, at a Hebrew University of Jerusalem course given at Empire State College, I also began to understand the historical and cultural aspects of many of the biblical incidents. The Bible began to emerge not only as a spiritual guide but also as the development of a particular culture in a difficult and contentious part of the world. Understanding the geography of the Bible, and something of the history of its peoples, I wanted to know more about the individuals. How did they live? How did they love? Ruth and Joseph and Lot became more than representatives of a distant mythology — they began to emerge as real flesh-and-blood people.

What's more, I began to understand the motivation for their actions not as reactions to an angry God or fear of divine retribution, but as aspects of love. What is more touching than Ruth's love and devotion to Naomi? What love could be so complete as Abraham's when he is to sacrifice his son at God's bidding? Viewed in this manner, the stories took on new meaning for me.

Rereading the stories from the Old Testament and letting them inhabit my imagination for the months prior to writing my version of them was a happy and illuminating experience for me. So was reading the Bible commentary of modern-day scholars who have examined the texts and translations and brought new insights into our understanding of the Old Testament and what it was like to struggle with what was then a relatively new religion.

I particularly enjoyed re-creating the stories in the first person. It made me feel closer to the young men and women I chose to write about. Like many people, I was familiar with the stories before I began the writing process. Like many people, in discovering them once again, I found new life and new meaning in all of them. I loved them once and, in these retellings, have discovered that I still do.

A TIME TO LOVE

And it came to pass afterward, that he loved a woman in the valley of Sorek, whose name was Delilah.

Judges 16:4

I FIRST SAW SAMSON in the marketplace. His servants pushed ahead of him, clearing the way. I stepped aside to let them pass, but Samson stopped a short distance from me and looked in my direction. He was a beautiful man with a wide neck, and thick, muscular arms I could easily imagine holding me. His hair, wavy and black, framed his handsome face. When he smiled, my heart raced wildly and I quickly moved my headdress so he could see my face.

He strode boldly through the crowded square and

stopped directly in front of me. Our eyes met, and his
consumed me with their passion.

"Is there a name for such beauty as yours?" he asked.
He leaned toward me and spoke softly.

"I am called Delilah," I said. "It means 'She who is
poor.'"

"I am Samson," he answered. "It means 'He who shines
down upon the poor.'"

"You are so big, you block more sun than you allow to
shine down," I responded.

He laughed, a great roar of a laugh that filled the space
around him. I could feel it with my whole body. The people around him backed away. He took my hand in his, and
I wondered if he would ever return it.

"And to what lucky man have you been promised?" he
asked.

"There are dreams in my life," I answered. "But no
promises."

"Then I must offer you some," he said, looking deeply
into my eyes. "And I always keep my promises."

He asked where I lived, and I told him. I didn't think
he would know our poor section of Sorek, and by the way
he looked away, I knew he did not. He smiled again and told

me that he had many homes throughout the land, and that I would make any of them more beautiful. Then he took my fingers and gently brushed them against his lips. "Perhaps one day I will send a servant for you," he said. "Will you come?"

"Send the servant and you will see if I come or not," I answered, hardly able to breathe in my excitement.

It was that very evening as I sat dreaming before a dying fire, thinking still of Samson, that two soldiers came to my father's house. They were not as old as my father, but smooth shaven as was the custom of our warriors. They entered our house with too much ease, too much arrogance, and then looked about with a contempt that angered me.

My father asked them what they wanted, and one of them took a dark leather pouch from under his tunic and placed it on the table. With one stubby finger he pushed it over, and a gold coin fell from the opening.

"I am Haziah, captain in the royal guard," he said. "I come here to make your daughter rich."

"Delilah is barely fifteen, a child," my father said, glancing in my direction, and then quickly away. "What did you have in mind?"

"Samson, the Israelite," the soldier said, looking at me.

"You know his reputation in his battles with us. He has killed many Philistines. They say that he is invincible, and it certainly seems that way. Nothing defeats him. In his hands, anything becomes a terrible weapon, a sword, a stick, even the jawbone of a donkey."

"And what can we do to help you?" my father asked.

"Samson has strength greater than any man I have ever seen," the soldier said. "He also has an astounding appetite for pleasure. Today he discovered this beautiful child of yours in the marketplace, and even from the shadows where we stood, we could see the excitement in his eyes. If this girl —"

"Delilah," my father said firmly.

"If Delilah can win him over and somehow discover the secret to his great strength, she would be doing a great service to her country and to her people. And to make it worth her while . . ." The soldier lifted the pouch and let the gold coins fall upon the table.

"You will give her this gold?" my father asked. His eyes darted toward me and back to the gold.

"We will give her a hundred times more than is here," the soldier said. "Samson is a thorn in the very heart of the

Philistines. Your daughter can help remove that thorn. Or she can return our little offering. It's her decision, of course."

The soldiers left. My father looked at the pouch and then at me. "Delilah?"

"I'll think about it," I said.

"I know of this Samson," he said. "He's a dangerous man."

I turned away from him and put a bundle of twigs on the fire and watched them flare up. My head was spinning as I heard his footsteps leaving the room. There were so many things happening at once. I had been thrilled just to meet Samson, and now our leaders were willing to give me a great deal of gold to find out his secrets. They had called me a girl, but they had come to me as Samson had — as a woman.

I sat on the edge of my bed, lifted my robe, and put three gold coins in a row on my thigh. In the soft glow of the fire, they seemed almost alive. My family was very poor, and I knew the money would mean a lot to them. The excitement of it all intrigued me. Samson, at least twice my age, was both rich and famous. But it was his reputation as a ferocious warrior that was best known to my people, the Philistines.

. . . I knew the money would mean a lot to them.

Seven days passed before Samson's white-haired servant came to our door just after sunrise. My father spoke with the old man while my mother helped me get ready. Her hands, wrinkled from years of weaving and grinding grain, pulled at my robe, trying to make it fit properly. I perfumed my hair and shoulders and put on a silver ankle bracelet and earrings adorned with white feathers. As we departed, I could feel the eyes of the village women following us.

The journey to the outskirts of Jerusalem took most of the morning. When I arrived, Samson looked me over carefully and was clearly pleased with what he saw. We ate a lunch of fig cakes and cheese, and Samson drank large goblets of dark wine that dribbled down his chin.

"I think you were meant to fill my empty heart," he said.

"I am just a woman who is fascinated by the great Samson," I said.

"Just a woman? There is nothing more beautiful than your smile," he murmured, his lips against my bare shoulder, "and nothing more exciting than the promise of your love."

"You use strong words."

"I'm a strong man."

"Can you guess my secret?" I asked him.

"Do you have a secret? I could never guess it."

"Then I will tell it to you," I said, pulling him closer to me. "It's that when I first saw you, I felt suddenly weak. And now that we are so close, I feel completely helpless."

He moved closer to me and let his lips brush against my cheek. "Love makes us all weak," he said.

"What possible weakness could you have? You are bursting with strength."

"You see me as so powerful. But if someone were to bind me with seven green cords that have never been dried, even I could not break them. Then what good would my strength do?"

It seemed all too simple, too easy. I had arranged with Haziah, the captain of the royal guard, to send messages through one of Samson's servants, and this I did, warning him to be careful. Haziah, in turn, sent me the seven green cords. Two soldiers would lie in wait until I signaled that Samson had been tied.

The next evening, after Samson had drunk his fill of wine and fallen asleep, I carefully bound him with the seven

"And now that we are so close, I feel completely helpless."

cords. As he lay sleeping, I amused myself by kissing him one last time before giving the signal.

Haziah's soldiers rushed into the room, screaming and shouting. Samson awoke instantly and sprung to his feet, the cords falling from his shoulders like threads. There was a brief flurry of grunts and blows that soon became piteous cries as, one by one, the soldiers fell dead to the floor.

Samson's strength was truly amazing. I had heard about it but had never seen it before. He had become like some fantastic beast — strong, yet calm. I put my arms around him and clung to him.

"Don't be afraid," he said, pulling me against his chest. "When they attack Samson it is because they are tired of life."

That night I slept in his arms, listening to the sound of his deep breathing. I felt comfortable lying close to him, as if I truly belonged encircled by his great strength. I couldn't help but wonder what he thought of me. He spoke easily of love, but did he mean it? I realized that I wanted him to think well of me, I wanted him to protect me even as I tried to bring him to harm.

My feelings for Samson were new to me, and disturbing. I told myself to think only of what I had agreed to do, nothing more. If I delivered Samson to Haziah's men, I would become wealthy and my family respected. If I failed, I would forever be a peasant, grinding grain and drawing water for some sheepherder with foul breath. I would become my mother, an old woman who sits in the shadows.

The next morning, the servants brought us breakfast. It seemed we were always eating. Then Samson asked me to wash his back.

"But why do you play with me?" I asked as I squeezed the sponge, letting the water drip across his shoulders.

"Play with you?"

"The soldiers must have bound you with the green cords when we were asleep," I said. "But when they attacked, you broke them in a heartbeat. As delighted as I am that you weren't harmed, I also realized that you didn't tell me the truth."

"Cords don't bother me that much," he said, with a grin. "But new ropes . . . that's another matter."

I sent the message to Haziah, and he, in turn, sent me the new ropes. When they arrived, I did not want to touch them. The adventure had grown old. Or had I changed?

Samson was fun to be with. For me, his life was one of luxury. There was always something good to eat, always a musician to play for us, always servants to do our bidding. It was a good life, but I knew I could not live it forever. I waited two weeks for a day when Samson climbed the hills to hunt. He was tired when he returned in the evening. He went to sleep and did not move as I bound him.

He is my enemy, I repeated over and over in my head. I knew I was caring too much for him. I reminded myself that there were many reasons to keep my part of the bargain. What I did was not only for myself, but for my people as well. And there was the gold that Haziah had promised, gold that would make so much of a difference to my family.

For a long while, as Samson slept, I sat looking at him. I imagined what it would have been like if I were not Philistine, but one of his people. Perhaps he would marry me and I would be the head of the house, with servants to draw my bath and prepare my meals. It would have been delightful. But I knew that could never be, and as Samson turned in his sleep, I gave the signal to the waiting soldiers.

Again, two young men from Haziah's camp came at him, and again Samson leaped to his feet, broke his bindings, and destroyed them. The soldiers lay twisted and broken on the tile floor. I quickly turned away from them.

"My servant was ill, and I lay with her after you fell

asleep," I said. "I will never leave your side again."

"Samson does not need a woman to protect him." He laughed. He had a bunch of grapes in his hand and held them high over his head. He squeezed them slowly, letting the dark juice run over his face. I sat on his lap and caught some of the juice with my tongue.

"Am I like your other women, just someone to use for amusement?"

"You are very special to me," Samson said. "Don't you know that?"

"How do I know it?" I asked him. "You don't tell me anything. All I know is that you are the strongest man on earth, stronger than the strongest giant. Nothing stops you."

Samson put down the grapes. "Again, you mention my strength. Why does it bother you so?"

"My only strength is my love," I said. "And I thought if I gave it freely to you . . ."

"We give what we can give," Samson said. "I give you every waking moment."

"I give you all my trust," I said.

"If my secret means that much to you, then I will give it freely," he said. "My hair must be loose. If it's plaited in

13

seven braids and pinned, then I, too, am pinned."

I didn't believe him, but I knew Haziah was running out of patience with me. That very night I braided and pinned Samson's hair as he slept. This time, three soldiers were sent: two young men and an older, grizzled soldier. I felt sorry for them even as they entered the room. As soon as they fell upon Samson, he tossed them off. They, too, were dead within minutes.

When the sun rose, and the bodies were taken away, Samson was in the darkest mood I had ever seen him in. I wanted to run to him, to fall on my knees and beg for his forgiveness. But all of that changed when my maid came. I was sitting in the window alcove, looking at the garden below, trying to sort out my thoughts and feelings, when she gave me the message, her eyes wide with alarm. Haziah was now threatening to kill my family if I did not succeed.

Later in the day, Samson, still dark with anger, sent out a message to all the Philistine people. He would seek revenge for the attacks on him, and he would show no mercy on those who stood against him.

"I am a Philistine," I said. "Will you kill me, too?"

"Never," he said. "You are Delilah, and I love you beyond any mortal being."

14

"I am afraid," I answered.

"Afraid? With Samson by your side?"

I couldn't tell him what was in my mind, that if I did not succeed in finding the source of his strength, my family would be killed, and perhaps I as well. Nor could I tell him what was in my heart, that I had grown to love him. "Yes," I said. "I am afraid."

"Then come tremble in my arms. In your sweet embrace even an angry Samson forgets his troubles."

"You don't even trust me," I said, forcing the words out. "I don't blame you. There's been bad blood between your people and mine for so long. I just hoped that one day, in the name of love, we could confide in each other. That we would really be in love."

"I do love you," Samson whispered.

"You want to," I said. "Your eyes love me, but your heart turns away. You don't trust me. I won't ask the secret of your strength again, Samson. But I will ask you for one favor."

"And it will be granted," he answered.

"If you kill me, please do it quickly so I won't have to suffer."

Samson buried his face in his hands. I knew I had hurt

him, and I knew, at that moment, that he really did love me.

He turned away from me, breathed deeply, and shook his head. I put my arms around his waist and held him tightly. *I love you, Samson.* The words filled my mind, and I wanted to sing them to him, but I couldn't. I knew I couldn't let myself surrender to the emotions flooding my body. Samson put my hands together and enfolded them in his own. "Delilah, tell me what you want of me." His voice was deep and husky.

"Your strength makes us strangers," I said. "It locks your heart from mine."

Samson sighed heavily. "Delilah, I am a Nazarite," he said. "I was born with a promise to God that I am sworn to fulfill. My hair is a symbol of that promise and must never be cut. My power lies in the strength God has given me to complete my mission."

There were tears running down his face and I knew, at last, that he was telling me the truth. I kissed away his tears and pulled his face to my bosom. "Samson, I love you," I said. "I love you. I love you. I love you."

I did love him, but I was no longer simply Delilah, the girl Samson had met at the marketplace. Now I was Delilah, the woman who must betray him.

"Come, let us lie down," I said.

Samson held me for a long time, and then, seemingly restless in that place between waking and sleep, turned away. I fought back the tears as I listened to his breathing grow more and more relaxed.

Samson, I am as weak as you are strong. Forgive me.

When I was sure Samson was asleep, I rose as quietly as I could. My maid dozed in the corner. I shook her gently and told her to bring the shears. She did so and, as Samson slept, as gently as I could, I cut his hair.

When I had finished I sent for the soldiers that were now always stationed nearby. Again, three men came.

"He is yours," I said.

I watched from behind the curtained window as they leaped upon Samson. He awoke instantly and tried to throw them off. But they bound him easily while he kept looking down at his arms and hands. I knew he must be wondering why he could not push away his enemies, or break the bindings that held him.

The soldiers danced in glee and slapped Samson about. His face was childlike in surprise as they dragged him away. When they had gone, I collapsed on the floor, my stomach retching in anguish, my hands shaking in anger and sorrow.

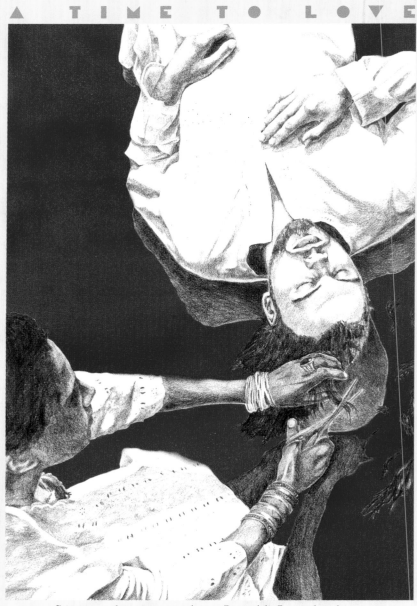

. . . as Samson slept, as gently as I could, I cut his hair.

Samson. O my Samson. What have they done to you? What have I done to you?

When I returned home I saw my father already counting the money the soldiers had brought. I couldn't bear to look at him, hunched over the low bench, lost in the pleasure of handling so much gold.

I heard that at the prison they tortured Samson and worked him from the rising of the sun until its setting each day. Even worse, they put out his eyes. It was weeks before I could bring myself to go to the courtyard. My heart ached as the others laughed.

"He is like a beast!" a woman said. "No more than a donkey."

She went to him and spit on his blind face as he neared her. I wanted to run and pull her away, but I dared not. I stood silently and watched as Samson moved slowly away, the ropes around his shoulders, his huge legs pushing forward in his thankless task. But then I saw something that I wondered if the others had seen, or if they had, knew of its significance. Samson's hair was growing back!

When I returned to the courtyard that night, I brought a handful of silver coins with me. The guard looked at me and asked me why I wanted to see Samson at night.

"It amuses me to see him," I said. "But Haziah does not want me to mingle with the common crowd that comes in the day."

He shrugged and opened the door to Samson's cell, but not before taking the silver coins I pressed into his palm.

I walked into the cell. Samson was sitting in the corner, facing the wall. As I neared him, his head moved up and he turned.

There were no eyes to look into, no clear dark pools in which to search for a soul that loved me. There were only two white, blood-streaked orbs in a face still cruelly handsome.

"Delilah!"

"You see me?" I stopped in my tracks.

"I sense you," he said. "Your scent speaks your name."

"If I draw near, will you kill me?" I asked.

"I might," he said, "if I can find your throat."

I drew near. He was still sitting, and I pulled his face against my stomach. Samson put his hands on my hips and slid them slowly up my body until he reached my throat. He held them there for a long while, and then moved them slowly higher, caressing my cheeks with his palms, now hard and calloused.

"Delilah." He called my name as a child calls for his parents in the dark. "Delilah."

Each night I came to see him. He would put his arms around me as I would first loosen, and then braid his hair. How quickly it grew. Sometimes he asked me questions. Were the olive trees still silver in the moonlight? Did the wings of blackbirds still look green as they turned lazily in the afternoon sun? At other times he would only pray, asking his God for forgiveness.

How could I see the olive trees when each night I cried myself to sleep? What did birds mean when all I saw flying before me was my own despair and that of Samson?

I braided his hair each night, but my heart stopped when it was announced that Samson would be tried for his offenses against Philistia.

"Where will the trial be held?" Samson asked.

"At the courthouse," I said. "But it is a mock trial. They want to make sport of you, to laugh at your weakness."

"At the courthouse?" he asked. "I have seen it. It is large and has carved pillars holding it up."

"I will speak for you," I said. "I will tell them you were a warrior and should be given a warrior's death."

"When they take me to the court" — Samson's voice

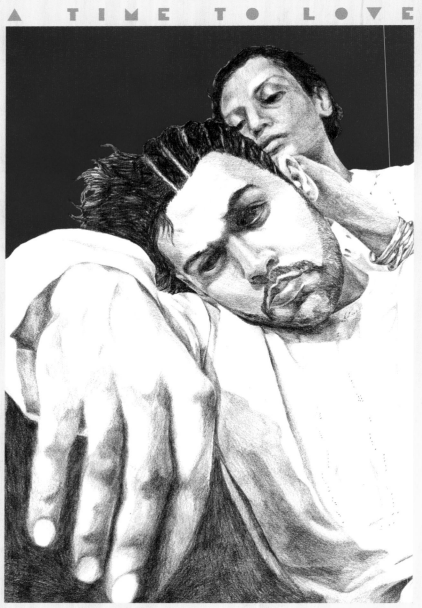

Each night I came to see him.

was low — "do not come to see me."

"Samson, I must be there," I said.

"God is with me, Delilah. He is all I need."

"How do you know He is with you?" I asked.

"I feel His presence in your hands."

"Samson." I put his hands on my shoulders and knelt before him. My voice broke as I spoke. "I have killed you, my darling. I have killed you!"

"It is not Delilah but Samson who has betrayed himself and his vows," he said, taking my head in his hands. "And it is Samson who sits here and sees the sweet light of redemption."

I moved his hands to my face so he could feel my tears. He smiled as he wiped them away.

The trial was meant to be more of a mockery than I had ever imagined. The judges led a goat to the center of the great room and announced that it would speak for Samson. The peals of laughter echoed through the high ceilings.

"Speak, O wise and mighty horned one!" a fat man from the government called out. "Tell us of his defense."

The people laughed. They laughed louder as they

turned Samson around and around until he grew dizzy and staggered, blind and alone in the midst of their derision.

"Let me steady myself! Please!" he called out. "Let me touch the pillars so I might steady myself."

I saw the boy put Samson's hands against the pillars that held up the roof, and I knew what was to come.

For the first time, I was no longer afraid, not of Haziah, nor of his soldiers. My only fear was that Samson would die with contempt for me, or worse, that I would not be there at all. I saw him lift his face to the heavens and call out one last time. As the walls cracked and the ceilings began to fall on the screaming crowd that raced past me toward the doors, I saw that all that he had lost was now his again.

My heart filled with love and terror. I looked at Samson, saw the bliss on his face, and knew that in this bitter end, all was well.

REUBEN TIME AND TO LOVE JOSEPH

Reuben said unto them, Shed no blood but cast him into this pit that is in the wilderness . . .   Genesis 37:22

MY BROTHER LIVES. Like a man risen from the dead, he has appeared from the ashes of memory. He tells us that we are to go home tomorrow and tell our father the good news. But that good news, the joyous celebration he envisions, is filled with danger and disgrace for the messengers. Grief and fear sit in the pit of my stomach like two huge rocks. If I could scream silently, I would do so. If my tears could speak, I would let them.

I have been tossing and turning all night. Sleep comes now and again, but then I quickly wake, my heart pounding.

The room is too warm, and I hear the breathing of my brothers who lie on mats around me. In the corner, the soft glow of an oil lamp throws a circle on the wall. It will be hours before daybreak, but I don't want to sleep again. I have already had the dream twice.

"Reuben, are you awake?" Judah's voice is deep, raspy.

"Yes," I answer. "Can't you sleep?"

"I sleep, but it's not easy," he says. "Did you dream again?"

"No," I lie. I don't want to discuss the dream. Judah was disturbed when I first spoke of it, and since neither of us can interpret it, I think it best not to mention it again.

Judah grunts before turning over, and soon the even sound of his breathing is lost among that of the others. In spite of myself, I think of the dream again.

In it I am walking down a great road. It could be the road to Hebron, but I cannot tell. Suddenly there is a commotion behind me, and I turn. I see a figure headed in my direction, walking down the middle of the road. He is wearing the robe of a priest, and his face is a shining light as he walks through the crowd. People on either side of the road fall prostrate to the ground before him, struck with awe. Some lift their arms to him imploringly, others clasp their

. . . his face is a shining light . . .

hands in prayer. When he gets to me, I am alive with excite‑
ment and look to see who it is who walks with such majesty.
But when I turn my eyes toward his, I see nothing but a
shadow where a face should be. The air around me turns
suddenly cold, filling me with dread. The figure walks on,
and this is where I wake up, always trembling.

What can it mean? Why have I dreamt it twice?

My brothers mumble in their sleep. They are all trou‑
bled. It is two weeks since our father sent us from our land
to buy grain in Egypt. We came for grain but found reason
to tremble as well.

My mind goes back to a day, on the very edge of
remembrance, a day brilliant with sunshine, when my
brothers and I sat in a circle in the fields of Dothan. We
talked about nothing, passing the time as the herd grazed
lazily in the field. Off to the left of where we sat, two lambs
nuzzled hungrily beneath their mother.

"Look who comes!" Judah saw him first.

We looked in the distance and saw an unmistakable
sight — a figure dressed in a long white robe. Sunlight
caught the gold trim and made the linen seem luminescent
against the distant sky. Father had had it made for Joseph,

and he wore it as if its ornaments were truly a token of his greatness.

"Father thinks the sun rises and falls at Joseph's command," Asher said. "Joseph said that we would all be his servants, and Father rebuked him for it, but I don't think he meant it."

"That will never happen," Simeon said firmly. "I will never be a servant to my brother."

"You will if Father leaves him all of his lands and fortune," Dan said.

"There is no doubt that he holds Father's heart in those soft hands of his," Judah said.

"There is no doubt that justice will not let him live," Asher said, turning his eyes away from me. "One thing follows another."

"Reuben, you are the firstborn." Levi closed his eyes and tilted his head back. "Tell me, shall we bow our heads now, so that we are used to serving him? Or shall we act?"

"What can we do?" I asked. "Our father's will is our father's will, and only God can change that."

"It's not right, and there's not one of you who doesn't believe that. Old age has blinded our father. If Joseph lives, we will die as beggars," Asher said. "My pride won't let me work for him and still call myself a man. What would I tell a wife? That I am the son of Israel, a wealthy man, but I am not worthy to share in his blessings?"

Levi took a handful of grass and tossed it lightly into the air. "If Joseph lives," he said. "It is not *if* he lives. The boy lives. We see which way the wind is blowing, so we know which way the grass will fly. We will be forced to bow down to him in spite of law and tradition. As he breathes, we will serve."

"Joseph wears his pride like a crown," I said. "But his heart is sweet. We can't just kill our brother."

"He makes himself not our brother," Asher replied angrily. "He truly believes that he is destined for greatness. It is a greatness based on what he would take from us, his brothers. And what he would take from us, surely we have the right to take from him. How many are with me?"

My brothers spoke in turn. Their voices were quiet but filled with conviction. I felt my heart race within my chest and my mouth go suddenly dry. I knew they must have spoken of this before.

"I can't even think of killing Joseph," Judah said. "To kill him would be to deny there is a God."

"Look, he sees us and he stops and sits by the way."

Asher nodded to where Joseph sat by the side of the road. "He waits for us to come and greet him. His arrogance is so thick, I can taste it. I can smell it."

"We can't take his life," Judah said again.

"I agree with Judah," I said.

Asher put his arm around my shoulders. He whispered into my ear. "Your truth must be your truth," he said. "If you see Joseph above us, then that must be your truth. If you see yourself on your knees serving him, then that must be your truth.

"But if you see that we are truly brothers" — he pulled me closer — "then that must be your truth. It is Joseph who has put the bitter where the sweet should be, and it is we who must do what we must do."

"Can you kill?" I asked. "Are we gods who can lawfully kill our own flesh and blood?"

"It is Joseph who sacrifices us to his vanity," Asher said. "We only have to remove ourselves from the altar he builds."

I needed to think. I got up and walked slowly toward where Joseph sat, leaving the others behind. I knew that, except for Judah, they were all of one mind: to kill Joseph.

I understood how my brothers felt about Joseph. There

were times, seeing how Father favored him, that I felt the same. But there is something about Joseph, something strange and wonderful. Where, in my other brothers, there are tides of wisdom, in Joseph there are floods. This I see in spite of myself.

When I reached Joseph, he stood, the way he did at times, his posture erect, his shoulders turned at a slight angle toward me. I drew near and embraced him warmly. He was seventeen now and grown into full manhood. I touched his cheek, and his smile broke my heart. Where the others saw too much pride, I saw too much inno-cence.

"Why are all my brothers not coming to greet me?" he asked.

"You should go to them," I said. "You are younger than they are."

"They will come to me," he said. He sat down by the side of the road, careful not to dirty himself.

Joseph's face was handsome, almost as fair as a woman's. There was a power about him that all of us felt when we were near him. But I understood what he did not: that his brothers did not want to walk in his shadow.

"Your crown of pride does not become you, Joseph," I said. "Your brothers don't like it. Can't you see that?"

"I see that they sometimes resent me," Joseph answered. "That is their fault, not mine. Even Father says so."

"Father has humbled himself before the Lord," I said. "And God has granted him a long life. You should think about how he conducts himself and do likewise."

"Look, they're coming." Joseph was looking past me.

I turned and saw my brothers coming toward us. Asher led, and the others were strung out behind him. Asher held a rope by his side. I saw that Judah, still troubled, lagged behind.

Joseph put up no struggle when they grabbed him. I could scarcely bear to see the pain in his face. It was as if he couldn't believe that it was really happening to him.

In a flash, Dan had raised a dagger above his head, and I leaped to stop it in midair. Dan's eyes were filled with the heat of the moment, and his hand pushed against mine menacingly, but I held fast.

"No! Shed no blood," I said, grasping Dan's wrist with both my hands. "But cast him into this pit."

My brothers stripped Joseph of his robe, bound him,

Joseph put up no struggle when they grabbed him.

and dragged him to a pit in the underbrush. Then they roughly pushed him into it.

"It is done," Dan said. "We are all the better for it."

But from the pit Joseph called out our names, one by one. He called mine just as the sun drifted behind a cloud. I felt sick. My heart sat like a great stone in my chest as he called our names again. Then there was silence.

We sat away from the pit, no one speaking except for Asher, who spoke more and more about Joseph's arrogance. I could see the darkness rising in him.

"But what use is there in killing him?" I said, looking at Judah. "Let's just send him on his way. We'll tell him that he is no longer wanted in this family, that his leaving would be the right thing to do."

Gad, who was usually quiet, spoke up. "He would run to Father with the news before the words left your mouth."

"Let's not do anything in haste," I said.

"Reuben, if we must do evil, let us weigh it carefully," Simeon said. "We know you are torn, but we must have some clear path to walk. A rock tossed into the air always finds the ground somewhere."

My head buzzed like a swarm of angry bees. I didn't want to hear any more, or think any more. I gathered the water bags and tied them to my belt. Then I asked Judah to go with me.

Judah searched my face for a long time, as he had done since he was a child, looking for my wisdom.

"We need water," I said. "And time to think."

He took a deep breath and nodded. I turned and walked away before he had a chance to speak. I saw by his shadow that he was following me.

As I walked, the bags slapping against my legs, I told myself that Joseph, lying tied in the pit, would come to his senses and repent his conceited ways. He just needed to see how we felt and how he was disturbing the natural order of things. He hadn't seen that kind of anger from us before, and I hoped it would bring him to his senses.

As I walked, I told myself that Simeon would come to agree with Judah and me. He would lift Joseph from the pit by the scruff of his neck, demand an apology, then send him on his way.

"What are you thinking?" Judah asked, walking alongside me.

"I am trying not to think," I said.

I tried to turn my thoughts to scenes of understanding and reconciliation with my brothers, but an image kept

. . . an image kept flickering before me.

flickering before me. It was the nightmare image of nine knives reaching into the darkness of the pit.

It was almost dark when Judah and I found the well we were seeking. We filled the bags quickly, and Judah knelt and spent a few moments in prayer.

"Reuben, how will God think upon us?" he asked when he had finished.

"He will see eyes filled with sorrow and feet that stumble," I said. "But also hearts that do not withhold their goodness."

We started back with Judah walking ahead and me following, each carrying the burden of our own thoughts.

When we reached our camp, it was Simeon I saw first. He came and took the water from me and asked how I was.

"Fine," I said. "And how is Joseph?"

"He is gone," Simeon said. "We have sold him away."

I fell upon the ground and covered my face with my hands. Simeon knelt beside me and shook me roughly. Over and over he told me that it had been our only choice, that Joseph could not live with us in peace. He said that if they had not sold him away they would have surely had to do him harm.

I didn't believe they had sold Joseph away. In my mind's eye I saw him lying dead, a stain of blood dried against his olive skin. How could I let this happen? What would I say to Father? How would I answer the small voices howling behind my eyes?

But there were answers that had to be made. We who stood on the edge of the empty pit were still brothers. I made Levi kill a goat and lay its still warm body on Joseph's robe. I watched as the blood seeped onto the robe and then as Levi lifted the animal off of it. The robe was shredded, as if some wild beast had ripped it apart with its teeth.

As my brothers gathered our belongings, I emptied one of the water bags into a pot and washed the dirt from my hands.

When we reached home, it was my mother who saw us first. She waved, and I could see her counting us. Benjamin, our youngest brother, stood near her. When she didn't see Joseph she called to Father, who came out and stood in the pathway to our door.

"Father, we found this robe," Dan said, his hands trembling. "It looks like Joseph's. Has he lost it?"

Father took the robe and looked at it. When he held it up and saw the blood, he opened his mouth, and such a cry came forth. It was a piteous wail that tore the still air, that crushed hearts, that stopped time.

I felt alone and naked in my grief. There was no place to rest my eyes, no ransom of pity for my soul. What had I allowed to happen?

We brothers, we who had stood before our father with Joseph's bloody robe on that dark day, are now in Egypt, sent by our father to buy grain. The famine in Canaan pushed us here, and we have begged for enough grain to feed our people.

There was a strangeness about the man with whom we dealt, and at first we put it to his being Egyptian. We were given the grain and told to leave, but we were stopped by soldiers on the road and, filled with terror, brought back as thieves.

"But we have stolen nothing from you," I protested. "Only taken what you have sold us."

The man held us in the palm of his hand for a long time, asking us questions about our family, about Father, and Benjamin. We fell upon our knees before him and sought his mercy.

"You know us as honest men," I cried. "Let that be our bond."

"I know you also as brothers," the man said. "For I am Joseph."

We shrunk away from him, covering our faces with our hands. Could it be? Was such a thing possible?

"Do not worry yourselves that you sold me into slavery," he said. "It is God who has brought me here, and not you."

There was no mistaking the tone, the sweeping gestures, the way the shoulder turned as he spoke. It was Joseph who looked down at the pitiful faces that bowed before him.

"My heart . . . my heart sings with gladness to see you," Judah said, holding his head in his hands. "To see you well is God's gift to me."

"Come to me." Joseph held out his arms. "There is no vengeance in my heart for those I love."

Slowly, hesitantly, my brothers gathered around him, each eager to win Joseph's favor, each rejoicing to be relieved of his guilt. But how could I find relief? God had called my name on that bright day long ago, and I had

Slowly, hesitantly, my brothers gathered around him . . .

looked away. This was the bread I had eaten in secret and that now choked my throat.

"Joseph . . ." I took his hand as I looked for the words to beg forgiveness.

"Reuben, there is no need to seek forgiveness," Joseph said. "God is pleased that we are together again."

In silence, we watched the Egyptians pack our animals with the grain we had sought. Joseph made sure that we had fair weights and enough to eat on the journey home. He spoke to each of us and gave us each some souvenir.

"Break the news to Father gently," Joseph said after wishing us a safe journey. "Tell him again how much I love and miss him."

What will I say? O Father, come see your sons, clothed with shame and dishonor? Your Joseph lives in Egypt, protected by God and Pharaoh alike, and we wretched creatures now bring you our bounty of lies and deceits? How will he recognize us after so many years of deception?

The day is dreary. Heavy clouds drift lazily through the gray sky. The Egyptians eye us curiously. They are amazed at Joseph's forgiveness.

45

"If we could go back in time . . ." Judah starts, but does not finish the sentence.

Innocence is a road that burns behind the traveler — there is no return, only the ashes of what might have been.

We go on. We cross the borders of Egypt into our own lands. I glance back, looking for the cloud of dust, for the soldiers sent by Joseph to seek his revenge, but there are none.

"It is true," Levi says quietly, "he remembers us only as brothers."

I nod and smile at Levi.

As the animal I ride pushes forward, I wonder what God will remember.

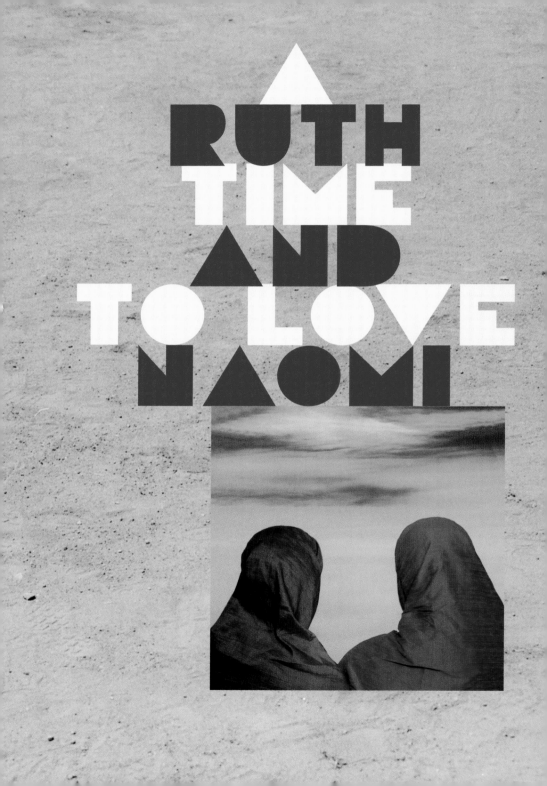

Where you live, I will live. Your people will
be my people, and your God will be my God.

Ruth 1:16

I AWOKE to the noisy twittering of sparrows. The
leaves of the wild fig tree above me were almost black
against the brilliant sunrise. For a moment, I imagined I was
a girl again, back in the olive groves of Dibon in my beloved
Moab. But the sight of Naomi sleeping a few feet away,
lying on her side, one hand resting lightly on Orpah's shoul,
der, reminded me that I was far from home. I did not want
to wake my mother-in-law, but I knew we needed to be on
our way before the sun was too high.

Orpah, my sister-in-law, stirred in her sleep and rubbed

one ankle against the other. I shook her leg and heard her murmur to herself as she awoke.

"Good morning," I said, speaking softly. "Did you sleep well?"

"I am still tired." Orpah raised herself onto one elbow and looked over toward Naomi.

"We're all tired," I said. "And Bethlehem is still at least five days away."

"If we were with a caravan, we could make the trip in three days," Orpah protested.

"If we were not widows, we would not need to go to a strange land at all," I said. "Our mother-in-law takes the best care of us she can."

Naomi, roused by the sound of our voices, sat up. "Look how bright the sun is," she said, stretching her arms before her. "It looks like a good day for travel."

"The sky is clear all the way to the mountains," I answered.

We took down the cloth we were using for shelter, and Orpah and I folded it carefully as Naomi gathered the food that was left. We were quiet as we packed, caught in the weight of the moment. We were nearing the border between Moab and Judah. For me, it would mean leaving behind the traditions of my people to wander into a world I did not know.

As we started our day's journey, I began to wonder what the people of Bethlehem would think of Orpah and me.

It had been years since Naomi, her husband, and their two handsome sons left the parched lands of Judah for my country. In Moab they found gentle rainfalls and rich lands. In Orpah and me they had also found loving wives for the sons. But that had been so long ago. Death had found the men, and misfortune the crops. Now it was Judah bursting forth with new life and Moab that edged along the dry well of starvation.

Naomi led the way. Orpah, small with delicate bones, was struggling to keep up. It was hard on all of us. Naomi carried her age well, but after merely an hour's trek, she had to stop to rest.

"You will be home soon." Orpah shielded her eyes from the sun as she spoke. "You must be excited."

"I am excited to have you with me," Naomi said. "With God's help, we will all be home soon."

We walked on, slipping into the silence that was now so familiar. When the crops had failed in Moab, there had

Naomi led the way.

been nothing to say. Our complaints would not make the wheat grow. It was the poor crops, fields of stunted plants, that had persuaded us to leave Moab and seek our fortunes in Judah's city of Bethlehem.

"What do you have there?" A heavy male voice seemed to tear the very air apart. We had happened upon the border guards.

"It is our belongings," Naomi answered.

The soldier poked at Naomi's bundle with a stubby finger. Another soldier, younger, with hairy arms and a thick neck, came over to watch.

Naomi sighed heavily and unwrapped the cheese, olives, and portions of dark bread we hoped would get us through the day.

"And where are you taking all of this?" the soldier asked.

"We're going to Bethlehem," Naomi replied.

"Why are you taking our food to strangers?" the first soldier demanded.

"We are not at war with the people of Judah," I said. "There is peace between us."

"You are a Moabite woman," the second soldier said, looking at me. "Why are you crossing the border?"

"These are women of Moab," Naomi said. "But each has married one of my sons, who have died. I, too, am a widow. We ask only for safe passage, nothing more."

"Our men are not good enough for you?" The soldier who stopped us pressed his fingertips under my chin and lifted my face toward his.

I caught my breath and held it.

"Do not . . . please, sir, do not harm her." Naomi put her hand on the soldier's wrist and slowly pulled it away from my face. "Surely we are no threat to such large men as you are."

"Let them go," the other soldier said.

The first soldier grunted, shook his head, then strode away.

We turned our backs to the sun and began walking again. Ahead of us, the dust swirled along the hard road as other travelers made their way northward. Naomi had drawn the route for us in the sands, and I tried to picture it in my mind. Orpah pulled her veil over her face. What was she thinking? Did her heart tremble as mine did to leave the faces we knew?

We walked until noon, and then a bit longer before Naomi stopped near a grove of small trees.

"We ask only for safe passage, nothing more."

"Are you tired?" Orpah asked.

Naomi put her face down in her open hands for a long time before answering. "The flesh is strong, but my spirit grows weaker with each step. I sit here and think of what Elimelech, my husband, would have said to those soldiers. And when I think of my sons, your husbands, and what life would have been like if they had lived, what fields they might have planted, I feel crushed with bitterness."

My thoughts went to Mahlon, my own young husband, and how strong I thought he looked when I first saw him in the fields. His hands were broad and powerful, the hands of a man who worked the land, but were so gentle when he touched me. At first, I had trouble understanding his accent, but his smile touched my heart in a thousand ways, and what I knew, whenever he was near me, was the depth of his tenderness. Later, when illness had consumed his body, and had taken away his great strength, it was the tenderness that we still shared.

When he first brought me into the house of his parents, I had been afraid. But Naomi had pulled me to her and uncovered my head, saying, "Let me get a good look at you, girl."

"I am honored to be in your house," I had said.

"My son has found more than my heart has wished for, my daughter." The word "daughter" left her tongue like a sweet song and filled my heart with gladness.

I don't know if it ever pained her that Mahlon had not found a wife among his own people, but I know that she opened her heart completely to me, as she later did to Orpah. There was never a sideways glance, never a moment in which I saw anything but trust in her eyes.

When Mahlon died, I thought my heart would die with him. It was Naomi who held me to her bosom and whispered in my ear that life would go on, and that we would have to endure. Not that I, not that she, but that we would have to endure.

Now it was I who whispered to my mother-in-law, "Bethlehem is not that far away. And somehow, we will make it."

"The distance is longer than the road, Ruth," Naomi said. "The way the soldiers of Moab feel about me, their hard eyes, their suspicions, is what my people are going to feel for you. It's a terrible thing, but it's the way of the world." Her eyes filled with tears.

"What are we to do?" Orpah asked.

Naomi tilted her head to one side and sighed heavily.

Her face, browned by years of sun, was now finely wrinkled, as if someone had placed a fragile lace across it. "The more I think, the more shadows I see," she said. "Both of you deserve so much. You've been good wives to my sons, and all that I could have wanted in daughters. I wonder if you would not be better off in Moab."

"Naomi, dear Naomi. My heart would burst before my lips could ever say good-bye to you," I said. "You are my mother now."

"We will go with you to your people," Orpah said. "There is so little for us in Moab. We have made our choice."

Naomi held out her arms, and we fell into them and she held us close. Our tears came like a sudden flood. It was the first time I had cried since we had started, and I clung to Naomi almost desperately. I was not nearly as brave as I'd hoped I would be. Doubts that I had ignored in my bosom now rose to my throat.

Naomi let us cry. When we had finished, she stood and turned toward Bethlehem. We followed.

The coolness of night brought with it the gentle scent of flowering myrtle. Exhausted, I longed for sleep. We found a small brook and washed our feet in it before laying

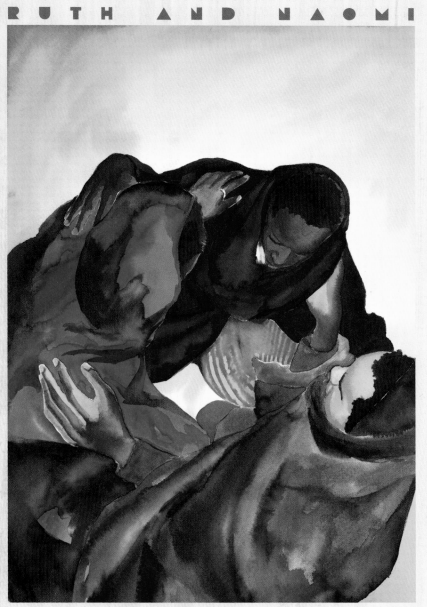

Our tears came like a sudden flood.

ourselves down to rest for the night. I dreamt I was working in a field. Ahead of me, a man was sowing seeds, and I walked behind him, covering them. From the man's back I knew he was Mahlon.

I thought if he had given me a son it would have been good. In Judah, I would have neither son nor daughter in my life, nor even the comfort of a husband.

By the next day all joy had left us. We had reached the sea, but the distance ahead still seemed endless. Time and again, like three brooding ravens, we rested by the side of the road that edged the water. A family that rested near us spoke of how good the crops would be near Bethlehem.

"Even the promise of a good harvest fails me," Naomi said. "I went out full, and the Lord hath brought me home again empty. I have to beg my heart to rise against the sorrow it feels."

I wondered if my heart, too, would harden. At a time when women of my age were cradling their babies and tending their own gardens, I had become a barren field.

When we were away from Naomi, Orpah spoke to me of her fears. "If her God has turned His back on her, what will He do for us?" she said.

The next day it rained, and the wind punished us with

its fury. We looked for shelter. Naomi spotted a small cluster of tents, and we headed toward them. When we reached them, she asked if we might come in from the rain.

"Who are your people?" a man quickly replied.

"I am Naomi, widow of Elimelech, of the tribe of Judah. These daughters are the widows of my sons."

"And who are they?" an elderly man spoke.

"Women of peace," Naomi said, "from the land of Moab."

"You are welcome here," the elder said. "But only you."

We begged Naomi to go inside the tents, but she refused. We huddled under a tree, shivering in the cold rain. The storm lasted for hours, and when it subsided, we again felt defeated.

"It is your God telling us that we are not welcome in the land of Judah," Orpah said. "Your people don't want us under their tents or under their skies." There was no bitterness in Orpah's voice, but there was pain.

Naomi touched her cheek, but Orpah turned away.

We dried ourselves as best we could, ate the last of the figs we had gathered, and were about to start again, when Naomi asked us to sit for a moment. She took a hand of each of us, and we formed a circle.

"Daughters, you must go back to your own people,"

she said, her voice quivering as she spoke. "It breaks my heart to turn away from you, but I can't think of anything else to do. If I could, I would have more sons for you to marry. But I can't. And if by some miracle I did, how long would you have to wait for them to become men?

"All of my good fortune is in the past," she said. "There is nothing for me now but to cling to my people with the hope that someone will take pity on me and allow me enough food to live. If you stay with me, then my misery will be yours. You are both young; you deserve the joys of life, the comfort of a husband. Look, there, along the road. There are Moabite families, your people, traveling to their own country. Go with them. Choose the life of a young woman while you still can. There is nothing for you in my land."

There arose in my mind a raging storm, like a sudden desert squall, blinding and cutting its way through me. I could not see what was ahead of me in Judah, nor was there certainty for me in Moab. There were dreams that could be sought and memories that might with luck be spun into something fortunate, but the only thing I truly held in my heart was the echo of Naomi's voice and the constant warmth of her love.

I closed my eyes against the storm, and now opened them to look into Naomi's face. What I saw was the gentle face that had given me her son, her trust, and her devotion.

Orpah released our hands. She kissed Naomi and then kissed me. Her dark eyes flooded with misery as she turned and ran for the road.

"Don't be ashamed, my daughter," Naomi said to me. "There is no sin in choosing to be young, in wanting the joys of life. There is no disgrace in wanting to enjoy the comforts of your own people and your own ways. You are a good woman, Ruth. Go with her and know that I will keep you in my heart and in my prayers forever."

I looked to where Orpah had run. I saw her talk to the travelers, and then I saw one of them hand her a loaf of bread. They glanced in my direction.

I turned to Naomi and searched her face. It was a face I had looked into so many times, and so many times had found more love there than I had ever known, than I had ever seen in any other face or felt in any other person. What more could there be than this love? I knew where my heart was leading me, and where I must follow.

"Dear, Naomi, do not ask me to leave you. Please, don't ask me not to follow you. Wherever you go, I will go . . ."

"Nothing but death will part you and me . . ."

"My daughter . . ."

"Where you live, I will live. Your people will be my people, and your God will be my God. Where you die, I will die there as well and lie in the grave next to yours. Nothing but death will part you and me from this day on. Nothing but death."

Naomi took my face in her hands and looked at me. I had stopped crying, and now a smile came to my face because what I had held in my bosom for so long had finally rushed joyously to my lips. She took my hands in hers and gently kissed my fingers. "My child . . . ," she said. "My dear child."

The walk from the valley of Mount Pisgah to Bethlehem was long, but our steps were lightened by what we knew: that we would be together always, that no matter what darkness fell upon us there would always be the light of the love we shared.

I am Ruth. The lands I see before me are green and beautiful; they are the lands of my people. My God above me smiles down warmly, even as the sun smiles down upon the gleaners in the fields we pass. The hand I hold as we make our way into the bustling marketplace is that of Naomi. She, too, is mine, and I am hers, here in our city of Bethlehem.

A ABRAHAM TIME AND TO LOVE ISAAC

. . . For because thou hast done this thing and hast not withheld thy son, thine only son . . .

Genesis 22:16

THE ROAD in front of our house twists boldly through the town of Beersheba, and then wanders northward toward the distant mountains until it becomes a mere footpath. Abraham, my father, sits on his donkey, his gray beard heavy against his chest, his shoulders slumped forward. Behind us, the servants, one sullen, the other dreaming aimlessly, ride without blankets on their animals. The animals travel single file, each in the shadow of the one before it.

Weariness pulls at my shoulders, and I wonder how my father's strength is not completely drained.

It is the third day of our travel, an hour after sunrise. We are in the land of Moriah, and my father has pointed to the dark mass on the horizon that is our destination. As the sun burns off the morning haze, the mass lightens and becomes a mountain, its peak nearly purple against the cloudless sky. I know that at home my mother is awake. Perhaps she sits at the table eating a crust of bread.

When I said good-bye to her, she smiled and touched my face gently with her fingertips. She doesn't see very well and uses her hands to find the memories of things she knows.

"I am taking cheese with us," I said, "as well as bread and oil."

"Isaac, my son . . ." Her words hung on the damp air. "Take my love as well."

The sun has reached its peak and has already begun its downward climb as we near the base of the mountain. My father rocks as he goes along, and the donkey seems to have judged his steps to move with the old man's motion. From where I sit, I hear my father's prayers thanking God for the blessings He has given him.

The road is not well traveled, and I keep my eyes open

 8

. . . she smiled and touched my face gently . . .

to look for bandits. All I see are merchants on foot, their wares slung across their backs.

"The finest pots!" one calls, running alongside my father. "Only to look at it, my friend."

My father does not look at the offered pot. He continues his prayers, and the merchants, seeing that he is a holy man, do not bother him further. They turn to me, but I do not look at them. They go on. We go on.

"Stop!" my father suddenly calls out. His parched throat rasps like a wounded quail.

I urge my donkey forward until I reach Father to give him my water skin. He drinks slowly, some of the water falling on his beard. The clear droplets sparkle like jewels against the coarse hair.

"We are here, Isaac," he says softly. "We are here."

I look at the mountain that looms before us. From where we stand, we see only a narrow trail that tortures itself along the steep ascent. It is a trail for goats, not for men.

My father tells the servants to stay behind, that we will go and worship and then return to them.

The younger boy brings the cloth in which there is the knife and the rope for the sacrifice. He also brings the lantern that we will use to light the fire. The other boy brings the faggots, still bound with dried vines. My father takes them and places them across my chest. As I take them, I see his wrists, pale and thinned with age, protruding from his robe.

Sarah, we are to make a burnt offering to the Lord.

These were my father's words, half whispered in the stillness of the morning that we left home.

It is His will.

At the foot of the mountain, my father turns to me, examines my face carefully, and then turns away. Lifting the hem of his robe, the cloth bundle fast against his side, he begins to make his way up the mountain.

I follow my father. I follow Abraham, who is righteous and loving of the Lord. He is my father, and I his beloved son.

In my mind I say what my lips do not dare utter: *But Father, if we are to make a burnt offering, where is the lamb?*

The first steps are hard, but my father is strong in spirit, and he moves boldly, slipping now and again when his foot lands on a muddy rock, but pushing ever upward. It is as if he is climbing to heaven. At moments he is like a man possessed, gathering within him the strength of his years, mindless of the steepness of the mountain he must climb.

At other moments he is as old as the mountain. He looks down, his frail white shoulders sharply angled against the deep umber of the trail. He has chosen the hardest path up, but I follow. I am Isaac, his son.

I watch my father reach for a branch and try to pull himself up. The branch slides through his shaking hand, and a small noise of distress escapes him. His sandal comes off, and he glances down at it, then turns his face once again toward the heavens.

I gather his lost sandal and carry it perched atop my burden of wood. I am a young man struggling to keep pace with an old man. The pace is good. The heavy breathing, my pounding heart, has its own life as we struggle upward. But soon it is my father who stops, one leg on a narrow ledge, the other limp along the mountainside. I climb to him and ease past. I feel his breath against my cheek and I am warmed by it.

On the ledge, I loosen the ropes of my bundle and my father watches me closely. The loop I have formed from one end of the rope allows me to tie my burden around my shoulder, freeing my hands. I reach down for him, and he takes my hand in his gnarled fingers. "Be careful, Father," I say. "My hands are covered with sweat."

72

I pull him up to the ledge, and he tells me he is all right. I tell him that I will be his strength.

"The Lord will be my strength," he says.

Down below, the servants are looking at us from a distance. Their faces are bright in the waning sunlight, and they shield their eyes as they watch.

"Your father speaks to the Lord every day," my mother has said. "And the Lord answers."

"Do you hear Him?" I asked.

"In your sweet voice, Isaac," she said, smiling, "I hear the Lord singing a joyful tune."

My father has already started climbing again, and I quickly follow him.

He goes slowly now. I can hear his breathing. He touches his leg where it has been cut against a stone. I want to watch his every movement, his every step, so that he is not injured in any way. And yet, despite my looking outward at my father, now in shadows clinging to the earth above us, my mind revisits the beginning of our journey. The two of us were standing in our courtyard as he signaled the servants to start out. He had mounted first, leaning his body across the dark-eared donkey and, with a grunt, threw one leg across its back. I stood at his side, ready to catch him if needed. My mother's face was half hidden in the shadows of the doorway behind us.

It was then that the thought first struck me.

Father, if we are to make a burnt offering, where is the lamb?

Now it is growing cold. The wind sweeps dust from the ground and swirls it about our heads. I am tired, but I know I need to be near my father. His breathing shortens, and more and more he uses his arms to pull himself from perch to perch.

"Should you rest, Father?" I call to him.

"No, it is not necessary." He speaks without looking at me.

As we climb higher, there is less grass and fewer ledges. My father's hands tremble and slip from the rocks. The sound of his breathing is like that of a man drowning in air.

"O Lord, give me strength," he cries.

He calls to God from whom comes all strength and all love, and his thin legs move once again toward the top of the mountain. I come abreast of him and try to smile when he looks at me, but my face quickly turns into a mirror of his own. Our faces are covered with sweat, our lips tight from our efforts. He moves his face toward mine, his eyes, dark under the whiteness of his bushy brows, stare as if he is unsure of who I am.

"Father, your son's hand is ready to help you if you need it," I say.

He closes his eyes for a moment, then moves again, struggling with his load. We come to a level place, and to the right the climbing looks easier. I start in that direction when I see my father moving away from me. He has chosen the harder path again, one that will try his last bit of strength.

I look down. The servants, if I truly see them, are small figures huddled against a tree. I follow my father and see that the binding of his sandal has loosened. As we climb, a small speckled bird lands near us. It looks surprised to see us so high. It chirps angrily, and I see, on a rock jutting from the mountain, that there is a nest. My father sees it, too, and moves away so that the bird will not be alarmed. As we go beyond it, the bird flies away, content that its babies are safe.

There is a narrow ledge, no wider than my palm. My father has to turn his feet sideways to move along it. His face is pressed against the roughness of the mountain. I am afraid for him. He stops. I wait for him to move again but see the deepness of his breathing. Quickly, I put down the wood and start toward him. "Take my hand, Father," I call to him. "We can go back the other way."

"Pick up your burden, Isaac. We have not reached the top yet."

I retrace my steps along the ledge and retrieve the wood. When I turn back, my father has made it from the ledge and leans against the mountain. The veins in his neck are swollen as he gasps for air. Carefully, I cross the ledge and stop at my father's side. His clothes are soaked with sweat. He still has the knife, wrapped in cloth, and the rope. He has put the lantern down. I lift it and the knife and the rope.

"I will carry them," I say. "I still feel strong."

"What more can a man ask for than a good son?" he says.

He doesn't rest long enough but turns again to the mountain.

Father, if we are to make a burnt offering, where is the lamb?

My throat is dry. My heart beats faster. In the distance, the sound of thunder rumbles and there is a flash of lightning

Carefully, I cross the ledge and stop at my father's side.

across the darkening sky. And suddenly I know why there is no lamb.

My father is offering God his own body as a sacrifice.

If he cannot make the climb, if the spirit is willing but the flesh fails, then he is absolved. But still I must have proof.

"Father," I call to him. "Where is the lamb?"

"God will provide, my son," he says. "God will provide."

Suddenly I see it all. The veil is lifted, the sun brightens the horizon. I see now that I am the lamb that God has provided. My father is offering his life for mine. If he gives his own life on this cruel mountain, then God cannot expect him to give more. O my precious father. O my precious father.

My legs no longer ache, and my arms are no longer tired. The tips of my fingers, a moment ago numb from scraping along the unforgiving rocks, now grasp the mountain eagerly.

By the time we reach the mountaintop, we are both overwhelmed. My father shakes from his struggle, and I tremble with fear. A light rain rustles through the swaying shrubbery.

There is a flat rock and upon it we lay the wood,

spreading it so that the fire will grow evenly. At the side of the altar, my father places the knife, the lamp, and the binding rope. He stands and sucks in as much breath as he can through his nostrils.

"The wind picks up," I say. "It might bring a storm."

"The storm is already here," he says.

He kneels by the small altar we have built and begins to pray. I kneel by his side, my thigh touching his, my shoulder there for him to lean on. I listen to his prayers and let their fervor wash over me. O Abraham, my father, I love you. As he chants and sings the praises of our God, so do I. I want him to know, even now, even at this dark hour, how much I feel for him. When he finishes his prayers, he turns to me and takes my face in his hands.

"Isaac, my son, I waited many years for your birth. In those years, I depended on the Lord to provide."

"I know, Father."

"This day . . ." His voice breaks as he strokes my cheek. "This day the Lord has provided a lamb to be sacrificed."

"I know, Father," I say. His image breaks into a thousand pieces through my tears.

His hands shake as he picks up the rope to bind me. I put my hands behind me so that he can tie them easily.

O Abraham, my father, I love you.

Twice he leans against my back, sobbing his heart out. Twice he drops the rope.

I turn around and bring my hands close together. The rope blurs in my vision as he loops it around and then knots it tightly. Gently, his vine-thin fingers barely touching my shoulder, he leads me to the altar. I lie down, saying again those prayers that my father recited. This time it is my father who echoes each line as I speak.

I turn so that I might see him one more time. His face, illuminated by the lightning that now streaks furiously across the pewter sky, twists in anguish. I am afraid, I am so afraid. And yet the thought that pushes the fear from my bosom is the pain of this feeble old man alone on the mountaintop with his invisible God and his terrible sacrifice.

"I love you, Father!" I call to him. "I know it is God's will!"

"I love you, Isaac!" He screams my name as he lifts the knife above his head with both hands.

I look away.

There is a sudden swirl of howling wind and a deafening clap of thunder. I hear my father grunt and cry out. Once, and then again. I call to him frantically. "Father, are you all right?"

As the wind rose, it suddenly falls. As the thunder roared, suddenly everything becomes quiet. There is a voice, pure and unwavering in its tone, that comes from somewhere over my shoulder.

"Abraham, Abraham."

"Here am I," my father answers.

"Lay not thy hand upon the lad, neither do thou anything unto him, for now I know that thou fearest God."

The wind subsides to a gentle breeze. The air grows still. It is as if, there in the gathering gloom, the whole world softly exhales.

"Father, are you all right?" I call to him.

"God is with me, and you are with me, how can I not be all right, my son?" His smile, in the flickering embers of the fire, is radiant.

There is a scuffling in the bushes, and when my father unties my hands, we see that it is a ram that has been caught in the brambles. God has provided the sacrifice.

The trip down the mountain is full of joyous scrapes and wonderful bruises. We prance and fall upon ourselves like children at play.

The servants grumble as we head for home. The hour is late, and they complain about the sudden squall. My

He screams my name as he lifts the knife . . .

father ignores them as he rides upright ahead of me. I push with my knees against my donkey's haunches until I am by my father's side, and together, the half-moon breaking through the clouds illuminating our faces, we sing a song of praise to the night sky.

*. . . The angels hastened Lot, saying, Arise,
take thy wife and thy two daughters, which are
here; lest thou be consumed in the iniquity of
the city . . .*   Genesis 19:15

I AM ZILLAH, the youngest daughter of Lot.
Although I do not often speak of such things, I wish most
to make my life like that of my father, whom I love more
than anyone in the world.

Lot is a great man, favored by God for his righ-
teousness and favored by the citizens of Sodom for his
genius. It is a careful balance, the hard angles of this busy
city of traders against the mysteries of the Lord, but it is
one that my father manages well. He spends half of each day
managing the business of Sodom according to the customs of

our city; all else in his life belongs to God. For my mother, things are not quite so simple.

"I have a thirst for life that is not easily satisfied," she said as she patted corn cakes between her palms. "If I had my choice, every minute would be filled with music, and every day with sunshine."

"Father would not want to hear you saying that," I answered.

"No, he would rather see me sweating in front of a hot oven, doing the work of a simple cook."

"He looked to hire another servant," I said. "But he couldn't find anyone he felt was trustworthy."

"He is too particular," Mother said. "Do you need to be a saint to prepare a meal?"

"He says the Lord guides him."

"The Lord guides us all, but when your father manages the business of this city, and as a city elder he does manage it very well, he is not too particular with whom he does business."

"Everyone respects Father," I said.

"He still gets wet when it rains," Mother said, looking out of the window. "There's a storm coming. He'd better get home soon."

"I have a thirst for life that is not easily satisfied."

It was hours before Father came home. The day had grown dark, and the wind rattled the shutters as Mother helped him out of his wet garments. Soon he was sitting with his back to the fire, a heavy shawl around his shoulders. Saaria, my sister, had finished her weaving, and she and Mother went off to start dinner while I served Father a bowl of broth.

"Mother said you must have stopped at the market."

"I was visited by my uncle Abraham," Father said, his voice barely above a whisper. "He spoke of the coming storm."

"The rain doesn't beat nearly as hard as it did a while ago," I said. "Don't you think it will be over soon?"

"You don't understand, child. Abraham says that Sodom has turned its back on God, and if it does not turn back soon, it will provoke the Lord to come down like a storm to destroy this place."

A breeze — it must have come from cracks in the window — made me shiver. "Abraham is very wise, but he is an old man, and his senses are strange," I said. "Surely you can do something, Father, to convince him that we will be all right?"

"I hope so," Father said, turning toward the fire.

Mother and Saaria finished preparing dinner and served it. After Father blessed the table, I hoped he would talk more with Mother about what Uncle Abraham had said, but he did not, and we ate in silence.

Lately there had been a sadness about Father. Sometimes I would hear him mumbling his prayers alone in the darkness. At other times he seemed strangely distracted when my sister or I spoke to him. Now he spoke ominously of our city, in tones that frightened me. After dinner I sat with him for a while, and he put his arm around me, and I felt better.

Early the next morning, before the day grew too warm, Mother, Saaria, and I went to the marketplace. We bought fish and lentils and listened to the musicians who played their instruments in the square. The musicians sat in the shade of the buildings, while before them a young woman danced. She danced sensuously, her dark hair flying about her face, the gold bangles around her ankles creating a counter rhythm over the patter of her bare feet.

"Do you see how she moves?" Mother asked. "As if at any moment she might fly from the earth?"

"Father doesn't think they are good people," I said.

"I don't want to be a judge," Mother said. "I just know that I love beauty, and that dancer is very beautiful. There's nothing wrong with that, is there?"

"I suppose you're right," I answered. "Still, Father says we shouldn't have our minds on such things as music and dancing."

"We shouldn't mingle with the crowd," Saaria said. "There might be thieves about."

We hurried along, pushing our way through the marketplace, along the stone path that bordered the old cemetery, and into the square where our house sat.

We locked the doors, as we always did when the streets of the city began to fill. There were many wealthy merchants living in Sodom, but there were many thieves as well. There was talk of old men on their way from temple being robbed in the alleys.

Later, Mother came into my room and sat on the edge of the bed. She was wearing her favorite silk robe and had put on the jewelry she was afraid to wear in the marketplace.

"Where is your father's mind?" Mother asked. "He is acting so strangely. Has he spoken to you about anything?"

"He says that he is worried about Sodom turning its back on God," I answered.

"Sodom gives us a good life," Mother said. "Your father

has a good position. We can learn to deal with its imper-
fections."

The day went quietly, with me at my loom and Saaria
at her sewing. All day I thought of the city, and how it had
changed. We were no longer allowed to leave the house
after dark, or by ourselves. The stories of good people
being beaten, robbed, or even killed drifted on the wind
like foul odors. A numbing fear grew within me.

It was early evening when Father, supported by two
young men, stumbled through the front gate of our courtyard. Behind them a noisy crowd of ruffians shouted and
weaved their way onto our property. Mother told us to bolt
the shutters at once. Saaria and I ran from room to room,
closing the windows and locking them. I went to Father and
found him deathly pale, his chest heaving as he tried to
catch his breath.

"What happened?" Mother asked, all the time looking
at the two young men who had come into the house with
Father. "Lot, tell me what has happened! Who are these
men?"

"They are holy men," my father said. "Servants of God.
They are our salvation."

I heard the banging on our front gate and the furious shouts of the crowd that gathered there.

"Father, I'm afraid!" I said.

"There is evil outside!" my father said, holding his hands before him as if he were holding something in them.

I could feel the evil. It was like a living thing, growing bigger, pushing its way into every corner of our courtyard, consuming the city of Sodom.

"Perhaps they are only merrymakers," Mother said, peeking through the blinds.

"Look into your hearts, for evil is before you," one of the holy men declared. "Know this for your own good."

The pounding on the outer gate increased, and I heard it crash and splinter away. Next, the door to our house shook with the reverberations of angry fists smashing against the wooden frame.

"Lot! Old man, send out your visitors!" I heard a rough voice shouting. "Let us have those beauties! We'll teach them what a good time in Sodom is all about."

The demand was followed by a raucous laughter that chilled me.

"Go away! Go away!" my father's voice crackled in return.

At the sound, we rushed to the windows and, peeping

through the closed slats, saw that a crowd had gathered below. There were men and women and some children. They were laughing, but there was no joy in their laughter. Their smiles turned to hideous grimaces as they pointed at the house and clapped their hands. The smell of wine and sweat filled the night air.

"Go away! Go away!" my father pleaded.

The sound of splintering wood was the response. I looked at the two holy men sitting at our table. They sat calmly, their hands clasped serenely in front of them.

"Father, I'm afraid!" I shouted. "What's going on?"

"Lot, do something!" Mother called to him.

Father neared the door, his hands grasping his head in despair. "I have two daughters," he cried. "Take them instead but do not touch these holy men!"

At first I thought I hadn't heard right, but then he called out to the mob again to take me and Saaria.

"Father!" Everything inside of me was screaming in rage and terror! How could he offer us to this mob? Was I going mad? "Father!"

The door was partially broken through and hands reached in, searching for the bolt that held it. Father stumbled back and fell to his knees.

The holy men rose and went quickly to the door. They lifted their hands, and from their fingertips came a blinding light that sent the crowd reeling back. They lifted Father effortlessly to his feet and closed the door again.

For the moment I was saved. But my whole body was shaking. It took everything I had in me to pull back a shutter and look into the courtyard again. The crowd, still blinded by the light, staggered wildly about in front of the house. Then they began to leave, still cursing among themselves, still hurling insults back to our house.

Saaria and I were both in tears. Mother sat on a stool, leaning against the wall. I looked at the holy men. I wanted to thank them for saving us, but I was afraid of them as well.

Somehow we mustered the strength to check the windows again. Father began to pray, and Saaria and I knelt close to him as we had done so many times before. The sound of his voice was familiar as it lifted and fell in the darkness. It was familiar, and yet I felt, for the first time in my life, that I did not know this man. Instead, I clung to Saaria.

At first light, the holy men told us it was time to leave Sodom forever.

The door was partially broken through and hands reached in . . .

"It will take us hours to pack our belongings," Mother said.

"You must leave now," the holy men insisted.

"Lot, my husband, maybe things will be calmer tomorrow." Mother took Father by the hand and brought her face in front of his. "There is always a tomorrow and . . ."

"If we could wait a bit." My father turned to the holy men.

Then one of them, his voice clear and stern, spoke. "Lot, arise, take thy wife and thy two daughters, which are here; lest thou be consumed in the iniquity of the city. The Lord will send down fire and brimstone on this wicked city before this day has ended."

"You don't understand," Father was saying. "I am a city elder; I have so much to do here, so much to take care of before I can think of leaving."

Father sank down on his bench, but the men gathered us in a tight circle and put their arms around us. Suddenly we were moving out of the house and through our courtyard.

Saaria gasped as we felt ourselves rushing through the twisting streets of Sodom. The cold morning air, foul with the stench of stale wine, rushed about us. Men and women, still in the streets after the night's drunken revelry, howled with the delight of their own debauchery. The holy men pushed through them and onto the road that twisted through the mountains. On the side of the road was the dancer we had seen in the marketplace. She laughed when she saw us, a silvery laugh as light as dew upon a morning flower.

"Do not look back," said the holy men, now guarding us on either side. "There is nothing back there for you."

My head and heart were pounding as we rushed along. All the while, my father prayed, beseeching God not to desert him.

We made our way through the heart of the city, and still the holy men urged us on.

"God will overtake this wicked city," they said. "You must reach the safety of the mountains."

"Wait, wait, it's too far for me." My father was bent over, his hands on his knees, his breath coming in desperate, heaving gasps as he rocked back and forth. "I know God wants to save me, but the mountains are too far. Why can't we go to Zoar? I know people there, and it's such a small town. It can be changed for the better. God will be pleased."

The holy men sighed, then looked toward the heavens,

My head and heart were pounding as we rushed along.

now streaked with the morning sunrise and cracking like wet timber on a raging fire. We turned and started toward Zoar.

"Do not look back," they warned again. "Lest you be consumed."

The air grew warm, and above us a shower of fire flew through the air toward the city we had just left.

My legs were tired, and I was falling behind. As I tried to move faster, I looked up and saw Mother stopped in the road. Suddenly she was turning back.

"Mother! Don't!" I screamed.

A look of absolute horror filled her face. Her flesh drained to a deathly white, and in seconds she was a frozen nightmare on that barren plain. One hand was raised as if she were trying to ward off something that had reached for her. In her sightless eyes I saw the reflection of the fire raging behind us.

An arm came around my shoulders. "Do not look back," came the voice, almost too quiet to hear. "Do not let the evil into your soul."

In anguish and grief, I pushed on, no longer hearing or seeing. Thoughts flew through my mind like crazed bats hurling themselves against all reason, betraying everything I had ever felt before. The angry crowd, Father pleading with the men who had brought us from Sodom, and most of all, the last eternal look on Mother's face.

Ahead of me, already at the turn of the road, was Father, his head down, shoulders hunched forward as he walked slowly toward Zoar. He seemed so much smaller, so much less the man I had known and admired.

Nothing was certain anymore. Sodom was destroyed, and all of its people dead. The life I had known, the bustling city, the comforts, were all gone. All that was left was the confusion of who we were and of how long the pain would last. All that remained after the holy men left us were three tired souls groping in a newfound darkness and a woman unable to leave her past, now turned to salt along the ash-filled roadside.

. . . in seconds she was a frozen nightmare on that barren plain.

. . . And when he seeth the blood against the lintel and on the two side posts, the Lord will pass over the door and will not permit the destroyer to come into your houses to smite you.

Exodus 12:23

THE DAY was unbearably hot. I was tired and hungry. My people pushed wearily through the fields of barley, and I walked with them, pulling the weeds from between the stalks. Now and again, when the guards were not watching, I looked across the shimmering fields and saw the white sails of the feluccas as they glided along the dark waters of the Nile. It was nearly midday and, shielding my eyes from the sun, I looked at the hill on the far side of the fields for my friend Gamiel. There were several figures on the hillside, and I couldn't be sure he was there.

When we were young we used to play together in his courtyard, never minding that I was a Hebrew and he an Egyptian. We would hide from his sister and tease her until his mother came and bribed us with sweets. Then we were children, happy with our games. Now we were both four-teen, and Gamiel had told me he might join the Pharaoh's army.

The guard signaled that it was time for rest, and around me people collapsed in their tracks. My mother was only a short distance away, and I went to her, wet a cloth with the water I had been saving, and wiped her face.

"Here comes your friend," she said, looking past me.

I turned to see Gamiel, brown as a nut, striding through the field. He stopped a few feet from me and tried to put on a serious face.

"So, are you working hard?" he asked. He squatted and sat on his heels.

"We always work hard," I said, squatting next to him. "It is the Egyptians who grow fat and lazy. Do you know how many fat Egyptians I saw in the market last week?"

"We are fat because our gods favor us," Gamiel said. "And your gods don't care about you."

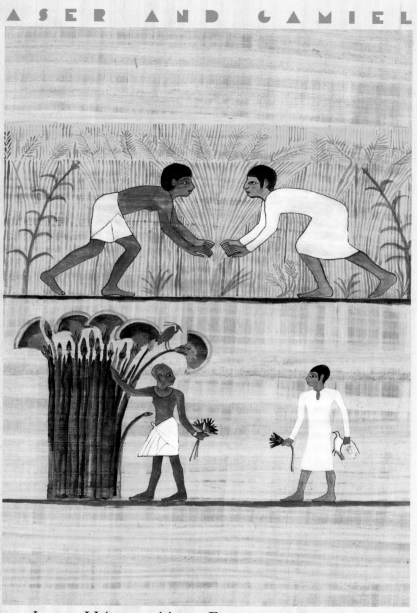

. . . I was a Hebrew and he an Egyptian.

"We have only one God," I said. "And He doesn't like fat people."

"How are you doing, my little friend?" he asked.

Gamiel took a small bundle from beneath his tunic and passed it to me. I put it in my sleeve.

"I'm doing all right," I said. "I'm thinking next week I might buy a chariot and drive around all day instead of working in the fields. What do you think?"

"We could both have chariots," Gamiel said. "Except mine would be faster than yours because my horses would be Egyptian."

A gentle breeze rose, and we closed our eyes and let it wash over our faces. Behind us an old woman sang softly to herself.

"Do you know what my mother said about you?" Gamiel asked. "She said when we used to play together you were as pretty as a girl."

"You tell your mother the next time she has a message for me she should wrap it in one of her delicious cakes and send it right to my face!" I answered. "I'm surprised you speak of me."

"It's hard not to think of someone who has been almost

a brother to me for so long. Sometimes I wonder what our lives would be like if you were Egyptian."

"Since the only thing I listen to these days is my stomach," I said, "I think we would be having a feast somewhere."

When Gamiel laughed, he laughed with his whole face. He had a wide, toothy smile and black eyes that crinkled at the corners.

"I am the firstborn of my family," he said. "And I would tell you what to do. Maybe I would have both of us join the army."

"I don't want to be a soldier," I answered. "I'll grow olives."

"We can grow olives for half the year and fight the other half," Gamiel said. "And when we're away we can have our servants take care of the olives."

"They're going back to work." I watched as the others began to take their positions again. The guard, a wiry man with a limp, motioned with his hands that we should all be on our feet.

"Will you come by tonight?" Gamiel asked.

"I don't think so. Moshe's brother Aaron is going to speak with the elders again. When he or Moshe speaks, we all must stay inside."

"My father says that Moshe does not respect Pharaoh," Gamiel answered. "He says that his words are so arrogant, they have trouble leaving his mouth."

"Moshe speaks the word of God," I said.

We touched palms, and I watched as he left the field. I felt sorry for him. I knew his heart, and it was not the cold heart of Pharaoh, it was the heart of my friend.

Two years before, Gamiel had saved my life. We had gone swimming, and I got caught in some weeds beneath the water. I had thrashed about, frantically trying to pull myself free. I had already swallowed too much water by the time Gamiel got to me and helped me free myself. Afterward, we rested on the shore, and he sat with me until I had thrown up all the water.

But that had been before Moshe had gone to Pharaoh demanding that all of our people be allowed to leave Egypt.

It was said that Moshe had asked God to cause the frogs to leave the waters and enter the fields, making a nuisance of themselves. The Egyptian magicians had also made frogs leave the water to show how easy a trick it was. Still, Pharaoh had said that he would let the Hebrews go, just to get rid of us, but there were many Egyptians who spoke against it.

"It would look like Pharaoh was bowing down before the Hebrew God!" Gamiel's father said.

My father said that the Egyptians wanted us working in the fields, so that they could grow rich while we suffered.

But when God made the gnats appear, and then the flies, it was the Egyptians who suffered. Then they turned their anger on us.

"Get rid of the Hebrews," an Egyptian man who made iron tools in our village sneered, "and you will get rid of half the problems in the kingdom."

After the plague of flies, there came a plague that killed many of the cattle and sheep. And after that came the terrible storms. They were frightening, sending rain and wind and giant hailstones that left the barley lying crushed in the fields.

But the late wheat was saved and harvested, and men from Pharaoh's court declared that it was the gods of Egypt who had stopped the storms, and that Pharaoh himself had saved the wheat. It was also announced that Pharaoh would not let the Hebrews go.

The Egyptians listened and shouted their huzzahs in celebration, but in every marketplace, around each village well, I could tell they were troubled.

▮ ▮ ▮

. . . there came a plague that killed . . .

"Why would you want to leave Egypt?" Gamiel had asked me as we sat behind his house. "There is nothing more beautiful than the Nile. I think in your little secret heart you know that, my friend."

"Gamiel, look at us," I answered. "We are slaves in this land. The Nile is not beautiful to a slave. The Nile runs freely; we do not."

"If the Pharaoh makes your people leave, you can always come and live with me," Gamiel said. "Of course, you would have to sleep in the stable until my father got used to the idea."

"If Pharaoh makes us leave, I will take you with me," I said. "And, of course, you would have to sleep outside of our tent until my father got used to the idea."

"Aser, Pharaoh is wise and knows what to do," Gamiel said. "He will free your people when the time comes. Believe me."

But it was Moshe who led us, and whom I believed. Moshe — sometimes distant in his manner, sometimes strange in his speech, but always with a passion in his bosom that lifted and rose like the tide. When I heard Moshe speak, he was a raging sea, a flood. To imagine him standing up against the great god of Egypt filled my heart with pride. God had sent down nine plagues to soften Pharaoh's heart, but every time it looked as if he would change, he hardened again, and kept us under his fist.

And then Moshe announced the tenth plague.

O my God, O my God. When I heard Moshe's words, they filled me with terror. There was never a plague to match this one, never a worse pain for any village to feel. My head reeled as I lay on my mat trying to think of what we must do. My head was filled with the suffering of my people, and yet my heart also spoke.

Quietly, I rose and slipped through the shadows out into the night air. In minutes, I was at his window. "Gamiel!" I called to him. "Are you up?"

The smells of garlic, fresh bread, and lentils were already in the air.

"Aser, what do you want? My father says I can't give you anything."

"Gamiel, I am afraid."

"No, you are stupid," he said. "Why did you come out in the middle of the night without a warm shirt? I thought even you had more sense than that. Look, you are trembling."

"Moshe says that God will send a terrible plague on the land," I said.

"Why are you whispering?"

"I am afraid God will hear me and strike me dead," I said. "I'm afraid to die."

"Don't worry, Aser, I'll take care of you." He put his hand on my shoulder. "Wait for me here, and I'll get something to put around you."

"No, don't go."

"Shh!"

Gamiel came back with a woolen cloth and a crust of bread. He put the cloth around my shoulders.

"Thank you," I said.

"You're trembling," Gamiel said. "Are you still cold?"

"No, but I have something terrible to tell you."

"What is your God going to do now?"

"Send death into the houses of all those who are not safe," I answered. "The firstborn child in each house will die."

Gamiel's eyes widened. "Aser, I am the firstborn. Your God is going to kill me?"

"Not if you do what I say. If you listen, death will pass over your house."

"When is this going to happen?"

"On the fourteenth day after the new moon," I answered. "Late at night."

I put my arms around Gamiel . . .

"Aiiee!" Gamiel buried his face in his hands. "Aser, you are my friend, but I don't like your God."

I put my arms around Gamiel and tried to think of words to comfort him, but I couldn't think of anything.

"Don't forget," I said. "You must do what I tell you and you'll be all right."

There was a feeling in the air, a chill that found the bones of everyone, Hebrew and Egyptian alike, as they went about their business. It went around the village like a thing unseen but that could be felt. People gathered at the well and spoke of it. They looked for signs from the heavens. The Egyptians lit candles and burned sweet incense.

"It will be the locusts again," an old man said. "It's what they do best, destroy what we all need."

Pharaoh, too, felt the uneasiness among his people and placed a heavy guard in front of the granary in case anyone tried to raid it.

We were made to work harder in the fields, and the guards were quick with their whips for anyone not keeping pace.

On the morning of the fourteenth day after the new

moon, I was put to digging a ditch along the edge of my village. Everyone around me was nervous. The other plagues
brought pain and distress, but this one would bring only
death.

I worked. My arms ached from lifting the heavy earth.
My hands stung as blisters rose on my palms. The time
went by quickly, as if the very day were rushing to begin its
appointment with God.

I looked around when I could, and I saw Gamiel. His
form was dark and thin against the horizon, but I recog-
nized the tilt of his head. When it was time for our break,
I moved away from the others so we could speak.

He brought figs and cheese and sat on the ground
before me. "Tonight?" he asked.

"Tonight."

"What should I do?"

I couldn't look into his face. "I'll put something on your
windowsill. It'll be a hyssop branch, with blood on it. Put it
around your door. On the sides and everywhere. Do you
hear me?"

"I'll have to think about it," Gamiel said. "My father
doesn't believe we can be in danger from Hebrews."

"Not from us, but from our God," I said. I lifted my

head and looked into his eyes. "Gamiel, it's not from us. It's from our God."

"Why are you crying?" he asked. "There's no reason."

But when I looked at his face, I saw his eyes glisten with tears, too, and I looked away. I felt him take my hands in his, and we clung to each other for a long moment. Then the guard came by, grunting and cursing. He stopped and looked down at us. I took a deep breath, let Gamiel's hands go, and said that I would see him tomorrow. "Be safe, my friend," I whispered.

Gamiel turned and walked away, leaving the figs and cheese with me. My legs were unsteady as I searched for my tools and started to dig again.

The sun was a huge red ball over the distant mountains. The sound of prayers, their solemn sweetness pushing away the gathering gloom, warmed our house. The smell of roasted lamb and garlic was everywhere, as was the sense of dread. My father, at the head of the table, reminded us of what Moshe had said, and we followed his orders. As the eldest boy, I helped my father, and after he had dipped the hyssop branch into the blood of the lamb, I took it outside and put it around the door.

Then, when no one was looking, I ran the few steps

down to Gamiel's house. I had whispered his name and left one branch on his window ledge before rushing back to my own house and closing the door.

I couldn't rest or find a comfortable way to lie upon my mat. I thought of getting up but didn't have the nerve. Each sound, each movement of the shutters, startled me into wakefulness. I thought of Gamiel, of the two of us sitting by the side of the river while he waited for me to recover when I had almost drowned. I thought of how close I had felt to him that day, and how close I had felt to him for so very long. I spoke his name in the darkness, and it gave me comfort.

I had almost fallen asleep when I heard what sounded like a wail. I closed my eyes and put my hands over my ears, but I could still hear it. It seemed to be coming from far away, perhaps near the village gates. Then I thought it was just down the path outside my house. It seemed to grow closer and closer. The shutters rattled noisily, and I thought at any moment they might burst open. "What is there?" I called out. "Father! Father! Help me! Help me!"

I closed my eyes and screamed and screamed until I couldn't scream anymore. I didn't remember stopping, or falling asleep. But I awoke in the cold grayness of dawn. My father was shaking me, telling me to gather my things, that we were leaving. I tried to talk to him, but he simply put his fingers to his lips and told me to hurry. Outside our window, the sounds of women shrieking their grief echoed through the village, and I knew they had found their dead and dying children. Somehow I got myself outside and half ran, half stumbled down the narrow passage to Gamiel's house.

His mother sat on a stool near his bed, rocking back and forth. Her mouth was open, but no sound came from her. His father stood in the middle of the floor, tearing at his clothes and sobbing.

"Gamiel!" I called to him. "Gamiel!"

"Aser." He spoke so softly, I had to bring my face to his lips. "Aser, I couldn't go against my father."

"Gamiel, I am so sorry."

"Aser, tell your God that I was your friend."

"I will tell Him a thousand times, Gamiel. A thousand times."

Gamiel closed his eyes.

The caravan stretched for miles. Moshe sent runners to hurry the stragglers along, warning them to leave any cattle

. . . the sounds of women shrieking their grief echoed . . .

that were sick or lame and reminding them that Pharaoh's heart had been soft before, only to grow hard again. Reminding them that they could not let themselves be too tired to pursue God's promise.

By the time the morning had blossomed, my legs were already aching with fatigue. The people around me pushed forward into the great desert. Some sang praises, others worried that Pharaoh would come after them again. I closed my eyes as we walked along and thanked God for the freedom of my people and for the promise of a new life.

Before saying "amen," I told God, for the first time, that Gamiel had been my friend.

ARTIST'S NOTE

by Christopher Myers

I HAVE NEVER SEEN the face of God, but because I am an artist, because I am about seeing, I imagine details. Two bright eyes, one the red sun of morning, the other a quiet moon hanging over the Brooklyn skyline. A warm, gentle smile, the wide horizon of the Atlantic Ocean where it presses against the open sky. Still, these pictures in my head lack something, some spark that would make them God.

In making the images for this book, *A Time to Love*, it was my job to try and find that spark. These stories that I know so well touch something in me, as they have touched something in countless people throughout the world. Who cannot feel the pain and anguish of a father stumbling up a mountain in order to sacrifice his beloved son for his God, or that father's relief to find that his God would not want to cause that kind of pain? Whether you call that father Ibrahim, Abraham, or Avram, there is a human truth to that story as well as in the other stories in *A Time to Love*. A truth that merits retelling, from the chisels of stonemasons

125

to the hearts of people outside the cathedral, from my great‑grandfather to my father to my brother and sister and me. These are truths that every artist strives to depict. My father has found these truths and new ways of revealing them in these stories. It is my job to capture these truths in my own way, through images.

My research for this book took me on a journey around the world (much of which is located conveniently in the Metropolitan Museum of Art in Manhattan as well as in the Brooklyn Museum). I wanted to see how other peoples had handled the problems of representing the unrepresentable. I traveled through gold encrusted illuminated manuscripts, through stained glass windows that told these stories to the masses of people who couldn't read. I saw wide‑eyed Ethiopian paintings, by both Christians and Falasha, as well as Turkish miniatures of the late 16th century. I looked at the work of Marc Chagall, Rembrandt, and Henry Ossawa Tanner. Through this journey, I discovered that all of these important images depict relationships between individuals and themselves, between people, and between humankind and God. This is the lesson of these stories, which my father and I hope to have shed some little light upon — God lives in our very human ability to love.

I found that though I could never depict the actual face of God, I could show where God is at work — in the quickening pulses of new lovers; in the calm acceptance of one woman for her daughter-in-law; in the embrace of brothers separated by class, culture, or betrayal; in the laughter of a mother and daughter talking in the kitchen. This is where God lives.